P9-DNA-856

THE PUPPY PLACE

SNOWBALL

ELLEN MILES

SCHOLASTIC INC.

New York   Toronto   London   Auckland
Sydney   Mexico City   New Delhi   Hong Kong

For my best pal Django

No part of this publication may be reproduced, stored in a retrieval system, or transmitted in any form or by any means, electronic, mechanical, photocopying, recording, or otherwise, without written permission of the publisher. For information regarding permisson, write to Permissions Department, Scholastic Inc., 557 Broadway, New York, NY 10012.

ISBN-13: 978-0-439-79380-3
ISBN-10: 0-439-79380-7

36 35 34 33   14 15 16/0

Printed in the U.S.A.   40

First printing, November 2005

CHAPTER ONE

Dear Mrs. Peabody,
Knock, knock! (Now you say, "Who's there?")
Isabel.
(You say, "Isabel who?")
Isabel necessary on a bicycle?

Charles laughed. He showed his letter to his best friend, Sammy. Sammy sat next to him in Mr. Mason's class. Sammy laughed when he read Charles's letter. But he also raised his eyebrows and looked over at Mr. Mason. Charles guessed what Sammy meant. He crumpled up the piece of paper and started over. It probably wasn't good to start a letter with a knock-knock joke, especially to a person he didn't even know.

Mr. Mason was a good teacher, but he was pretty serious. He had been teaching about the right ways and wrong ways to write a letter since Thanksgiving. Now it was almost Christmas, and everybody in Room 2B had heard it over and over again. "Say why you are writing the letter at the very beginning," Mr. Mason said. "And make sure to let the reader know who you are."

They had been writing letters for weeks, and Charles felt like he had already written a thousand letters.

Well, maybe ten.

At least five.

There was the one to the President. Charles asked him about how he had named his dog. There was the one to Holly James, his favorite writer. Charles asked her where she got her ideas, and if she had a dog. And there was the one to his parents. This letter explained all the reasons why Charles deserved a really, really good Christmas present this year. Like a dog.

Charles really loved dogs.

Now he was supposed to be writing to Mrs. Peabody, who was going to become his Grandbuddy. Every kid at Littleton Elementary was getting a Grandbuddy soon. Each class was going to be visiting The Meadows, which was a place where older people lived. Not sick old people, like in a hospital. These old people lived in their own apartments and took care of themselves, with a little help. But they might get a little lonely sometimes, and maybe their real grandchildren lived far away. That's where Grandbuddies came in.

Mr. Mason had given the kids in 2B a little bit of information about their Grandbuddies. Sammy's was named Mr. Munsell. Mr. Munsell had once been a pitcher in the minor leagues. Charles's information sheet said that Mrs. Peabody had been a librarian. That was okay, but not as exciting as a baseball player.

Charles decided to start his letter over, trying

to keep Mr. Mason's directions in mind. "Tell your Grandbuddy a little bit about yourself," Mr. Mason had said. "Your family, your likes and dislikes, your favorite food. And don't forget to ask your Grandbuddy about himself or herself, too. Have fun with it!"

Maybe Charles had been trying too hard with the "fun" part. Maybe Mrs. Peabody didn't even like knock-knock jokes.

Dear Mrs. Peabody,

Hi! I am going to be your Grandbuddy. My name is Charles Peterson. I am in second grade. I have one older sister named Lizzie. She is in fourth grade. I also have one younger brother named Adam, but we call him the Bean. He's little. We adopted him when he was a baby. The Bean thinks he is a dog and he likes to bark and drink from a bowl on the floor. My dad is a fireman, and my mom is a reporter.

Charles stopped writing and thought for a moment. What else could he tell Mrs. Peabody about himself? Mr. Mason said that sharing likes and dislikes was a good way to get to know someone.

My likes and dislikes are: I like dogs. I mean, I love them. A little while ago my family got to be a foster family for a golden retriever puppy named Goldie. A foster family takes care of a puppy for a little while. And they help find a really good forever home for the puppy, too. Mom says our family isn't ready for a full-time dog, but she liked having Goldie even though she chewed some stuff up. (Goldie, not Mom.) Anyway, it was the most fun ever, except when we had to give her away. (Goldie, not Mom.) The coolest thing is, the home we found for Goldie is with my best friend, Sammy. He lives right next door, so I get to see her all the time.

Charles thought for a minute.

I also like knock-knock jokes. I'll tell you one when I meet you. Hint: It's about a dog.

My dislikes: not having a dog of my own. And mushrooms.

My favorite food is: spaghetti, but I don't like meatballs. If I had a dog I could give him my meatballs.

Charles put down his pencil and shook out his hand. He had been writing a lot! The letter was almost done. Except, he had forgotten to ask Mrs. Peabody about herself. He picked up his pencil.

What about you? Do you have a dog?
Your Grandbuddy,
Charles

Charles looked down at his paper. He had written much more than he had planned to, and a lot of it seemed to be about dogs. Oh, well. The bell had just rung. It was time to hand in his letter, tidy up his desk, and line up by the door.

"When do you get to meet your Grandbuddies?" Lizzie asked Charles and Sammy on their way home from school. It was snowing, and Charles was trying to catch a snowflake on his tongue.

"On Monday," Sammy said. "I'm going to bring Mr. Munsell a picture of Goldie and Rufus."

Rufus was Sammy's other dog. Rufus was an older golden retriever, and he *loved* having Goldie around. They were always chasing each other and stealing each other's toys. Hearing about the picture made Charles feel a little jealous. Why didn't *he* have a dog he could bring a picture of?

"Charles! Lizzie! Hop in!" It was their dad, pulling up next to them in the Petersons' red pickup truck. He looked excited.

"Where are we going?" Charles asked.

"Down to Olson's gas station," Dad answered. "There's a puppy there. A puppy that needs a good foster home."

CHAPTER TWO

"Another puppy?" Lizzie asked. "What kind?"

"How old is it? Is it a girl or a boy? Can we keep it this time?" Charles was so excited he could hardly think straight.

Dad just laughed. "The sooner we get there the sooner we'll know more about this pup," he said. "Let's go!"

"You guys are so lucky," Sammy said. "I wish I could come, but I have to go home and take care of Goldie and Rufus. Call me as soon as you get home. I want to meet the new puppy!"

Charles and Lizzie climbed into the truck and fastened their seat belts.

"Okay, Dad, tell us everything you know," Lizzie demanded as they headed downtown.

"Also, does Mom know about the puppy? Is it okay with her?"

Charles was wondering the same thing. Mom was not exactly a dog person. She thought they were a lot of trouble and mess. She had promised Charles and Lizzie that they could get a dog someday — but that someday never seemed to come. Charles and Lizzie had felt really lucky that Mom had agreed to let them foster Goldie, the golden retriever puppy. Of course, they had hoped she would let them keep Goldie forever, but that had not happened. Maybe this time it would!

Dad laughed again at Lizzie's questions. "Yup, Mom knows. She's excited. So is the Bean. He's been running around yelling, 'Uppy! Uppy!' ever since he heard us talking about a puppy." Then Dad got serious. "Mom did say to remind you that we're just fostering this pup until we can find it a good home. So that answers *one* of your questions, buddy," he said, looking at Charles in the rearview mirror. "As for the others, all I know is that somebody left the pup in a box at Olson's gas station. I guess they thought he'd know what to do with a dog, since everybody knows Gunnar."

Gunnar was a Dalmatian and the fire department's mascot. He belonged to Bruce Olson, who was on the fire squad with Mr. Peterson. Gunnar was so smart and brave. Once he had saved a little boy by pulling him out of a burning house! Charles thought Gunnar was a real hero.

"But what breed is the puppy?" Lizzie asked.

Dad shook his head. "Bruce Olson said it was some sort of terrier."

Lizzie groaned. "Oh, no, a little dog?" she asked. Lizzie loved dogs as much as Charles did, but not *all* dogs. She mostly liked big dogs, like golden retrievers and Labradors and Great Danes. She always said they were "real dogs." They were dogs you could play with and throw sticks to and hug around the neck. Lizzie said that little dogs didn't count.

Dad felt the same way. "No such luck," he said as he pulled up at Littleton's main stoplight. "I think Bruce said the dog was white and kind of fluffy."

Lizzie rolled her eyes.

"White and fluffy sounds great!" Charles said. "It's probably really cute!"

"Right, and yappy, too," said Lizzie. "Oh, well. It's still a puppy. This'll be great. Do we have enough food at home? What about a crate for it to sleep in? Where are the toys we got for Goldie?"

"Mom's taking care of all of that," Dad said. "She's getting everything ready." He paused for a second. "But we're not going straight home with the puppy. First we're going to the vet. I already called and made an appointment. Mr. Olson said the puppy looked like it needed some attention." He pulled the truck into Olson's gas station, turned off the engine, and looked at Charles and Lizzie. "This puppy will probably need some extra care. Are you two ready for that responsibility?"

Charles nodded hard.

So did Lizzie.

Dad smiled. "I know you two can work hard when it comes to taking care of a puppy. You showed that when we had Goldie. Mom and I were proud of you. That's part of why we decided to foster another puppy."

Charles couldn't stand waiting another minute to see the new puppy. "Can we see it now? Please?"

"Sure," Dad said. "Mr. Olson told me he'd be waiting for us in the garage."

Charles opened the door, jumped out of the truck, and headed straight for the garage.

"Hey there, Charles!" called a tall man in blue coveralls. "Bet you're here to buy some new snow tires!" Mr. Olson was always joking around.

Charles shook his head.

"Oil change?"

"Where's the puppy?" Charles demanded. Usually, Charles loved to joke with Mr. Olson. But today he was on a mission. A puppy mission.

Mr. Olson smiled. "Right over here," he said, leading Charles to a quiet corner.

Charles looked into the big, dented cardboard box and saw two round black eyes looking back up at him. "Ohh," he said softly. The puppy was white and fluffy, all right. But its coat was dirty and matted in places. It had triangular ears — one that stood up and one that flopped over — and short little legs and a short little tail, and the cutest little face Charles had ever seen.

"He's a good boy," Mr. Olson said. "Hasn't even been crying."

"It's a boy!" Charles told Lizzie, who had just joined him at the box.

Lizzie peered down at the puppy. "It's a Westie!" she pronounced after a moment.

"A *what*?" Dad asked, looking into the box.

Lizzie knew all her dog breeds by heart. She had a poster in her room that showed every kind of dog there was and told all about their person- alities. "A West Highland white terrier," Lizzie said. "I was just reading about them. They're very smart and very energetic."

Dad looked doubtful. "This one doesn't seem too peppy," he said.

It was true. The puppy was sitting up, but it didn't seem excited to see new people. Its black eyes weren't shiny, and Charles could see that the inside of one of its ears was all red. It looked like it must hurt. The puppy gazed back up at them and lifted one paw, as if to say, "Help me."

The puppy felt so tired and hungry. Did these people have food? He couldn't remember the last time he had eaten.

Charles felt his heart go thump. In one second, he fell completely in love with the puppy. "We have to get this little guy to the vet," he said. "I think he's sick."

Mr. Olson helped Dad load the box into the

backseat of the truck. "Good luck," he said, "and let me know how things turn out."

Charles spent the whole drive to the vet staring at the quiet little puppy. He was dying to hold him, but he knew it was better not to take him out of the box until they got to the vet. "Do you think he's going to be all right?" Charles asked Dad.

"We'll know in a few minutes," Dad said. "I'm sure Dr. Gibson will know just what to do." He pulled into a parking spot near a big old house with a barn. DR. KATE GIBSON, VETERINARIAN, read a sign on the backdoor of the house. There were colorful Christmas lights strung along the porch.

As soon as they wrestled the box out of the truck, a tall woman with a long blond braid came out of the door. "I'm Katie Gibson," she said. "You must be the Petersons. Let me give you a hand with that pup."

Charles was glad to see the vet. He was so worried about the sick puppy! He hoped the vet could help.

CHAPTER THREE

"Well, well, well," said Dr. Gibson, once they had brought the box into her office. "What do we have here?" She smiled at Lizzie and Charles as she rolled up the sleeves of her flannel shirt. Then she reached into the box and gently lifted the puppy out. "Hello, little sweetie," she said as she settled him onto a soft, thick blanket she'd laid on her table.

The puppy liked the woman's soft touch and soft voice. Maybe this person would give him some food!

Charles bit his lip. The puppy looked so sick! It wasn't frisky and happy, the way Goldie had been. It just sat there, looking up at Dr. Gibson with sad eyes. "Is he going to be okay?" Charles asked. "Why is he so quiet?"

Dr. Gibson smiled. "I think he'll be fine," she said. "He's just underfed and a little dehydrated. That means he hasn't had enough to drink lately, so his body really needs water. Also, he probably has worms. Lots of puppies do. See how his belly sticks out, even though the rest of him is kind of skinny?" The doctor pointed to the puppy's tummy. "That's a sure sign he has worms. No big deal — we'll just give him a couple of pills for that and he'll be better very soon." As she talked, she was running her hands over the puppy.

"Worms?" Lizzie asked. "Gross!"

Charles thought it was gross, too, but he also knew things like that were just part of having a dog.

"This puppy will perk up fast," Dr. Gibson said. "Westies are pretty energetic little dogs when they're healthy."

"I *knew* it was a Westie!" Lizzie said.

"Good for you," said Dr. Gibson. "You must really know your dog breeds."

Lizzie beamed.

"I can't imagine why anyone wouldn't want such a sweet puppy," Mr. Peterson said. "There wasn't any note or anything."

Dr. Gibson shook her head. "It's such a shame," she said. "I suppose somebody just felt they couldn't take care of him."

"So they left him at a *gas* station?" Lizzie asked. She looked mad. "They should have brought him to the animal shelter, at least."

Charles knew that the shelter was a place where dogs and cats could stay until they found good homes. It wasn't as nice as staying with a family, but at least it was a safe place.

"You're right," said Dr. Gibson. "But maybe they did the best they could. Anyway, he'll be taken care of from now on. I can see that."

"We're just his foster family," Lizzie explained.

"Once he's all well, we'll be looking for a good home for him."

"I'll let you know if I hear of one," said the vet. "He should be ready to go to a new home within a couple of weeks."

Charles didn't say anything. How could Lizzie be so ready to give this dog up? His fur was so soft and his eyes were so black. Charles couldn't believe how cute the puppy was. He looked just like a stuffed toy, only he was real! Even if he was only going to be a foster dog, not a forever dog, Charles hoped they could keep him until the end of Christmas vacation. Once he got better, he would be so much fun to play with!

"We'll give him some shots, too," said Dr. Gibson, "just to make sure he's covered. I'd say he's about twelve weeks old, which means he's due for his final puppy shots." Now she was looking into the puppy's cute, pointed ears and checking inside his mouth. "He has a little ear infection — I'll give you some medicine for that. But you know, he really looks like a fine little pup."

Just as she said that, the puppy seemed to perk up a bit. He nuzzled her hand and licked it.

"That's the boy," said Dr. Gibson, laughing. "Does that mean you're ready for your shots?" She turned to Charles. "How about if you hold him while I get everything ready?"

"Really?" Charles stepped forward, and Dr. Gibson picked up the puppy and put him into Charles's arms.

"If you snuggle with him and distract him, he probably won't even feel the shot," she said.

Charles held the puppy carefully. "It's okay, little guy," he whispered as he stroked his fluffy white fur. "We're going to take good care of you."

Lizzie patted the dog, too.

He looked up at both of them with trusting eyes. Then he licked Charles on the cheek, and Charles could smell his sweet puppy breath.

"There! All done," said Dr. Gibson. Charles had

hardly noticed her giving the shot, and the puppy hadn't noticed at all. "Let's give him some food and water. If he eats okay, you can take him home tonight. Otherwise, I'll have to keep him here."

A few minutes later, Charles held his breath as the vet put the puppy down on the floor next to the food and water she had prepared. Would he eat?

Finally! Food! The puppy wondered why it had taken these people so long to figure out what he needed.

The puppy went straight for the food. In fact, he walked right into the dish and put his whole face into it! After he had eaten every speck of his dinner, he licked off his paws and his whiskers. Then he waded into the water dish and took a big, long drink. He sneezed when he was finished.

Everybody laughed.

"I think you can take this guy home," Dr. Gibson said to Mr. Peterson. She told them to give him some more water and some food when they got home — not a lot to start, but plenty of small meals — and see how he did. She said they might be surprised at how quickly he improved with a little care. "If you have any questions or concerns, you can call me anytime," she finished.

"Sounds great!" said Dad.

"Can we give him a bath?" Lizzie asked. "He looks so grungy."

"I think that should wait for a day or two," said Dr. Gibson. "But as soon as he seems a little livelier, a bath would be an excellent idea."

"Thanks, Dr. Gibson," said Charles as she helped him put the puppy back into the box for the ride home.

"My pleasure," she said, reaching in to give the pup one more pat.

When they got home, Charles helped his dad carry the box into the kitchen.

"Uppy!" yelled the Bean when he saw them come in.

"Better hold him, Mom," said Lizzie. "Dr. Gibson says some terrier puppies take a while to get used to younger kids. Anyway, this puppy needs to get better before he'll want to play."

But the puppy surprised them all. As soon as they put down the box, he tried to climb out! With a little whimper, he wriggled and squirmed and pawed at the sides of the box. Then Charles picked him up and put him on the floor.

"Wow, he's feeling better already," Charles said. He watched happily as the little pup began to roam all over the kitchen, acting as if he belonged there. Then the puppy plopped down on his little behind and looked up at them expectantly. He gave a couple of bossy little barks.

The puppy wanted the people to know it was time for more food. After he ate, he would explore some more. He thought this place was interesting. He was going to enjoy being in charge of it.

CHAPTER FOUR

Over the weekend, the puppy got better and better. Charles and Lizzie gave him his worm medicine, and they fed him lots of little meals. If they waited too long before feeding him, he would bark his high, short barks to remind them. They kept his ears clean and put on the special cream Dr. Gibson had given them. They made sure the puppy always had plenty of water, even if it meant they had to watch him all the time so he didn't "make a mistake" inside the house. And he never did — not once!

"I have to admit, this is one smart pup, even if he *is* just a little dog," said Lizzie. "Maybe we should name him Einstein, after the famous scientist."

The Petersons had been trying to figure out a

good name for the pup ever since they had brought him home.

Mr. Peterson thought they should call him the Sock Bandit, since he kept stealing everyone's socks. Nobody could find a matching pair!

Mom wanted to call him Snuffles, because he spent so much time sniffing everything in sight. He was very curious.

Charles was voting for Fuzzface. Why? Because of the puppy's fluffy coat, of course. That was more of a nickname than a real name.

And the Bean just called him "Uppy!"

But so far, not one of the names had stuck.

"How about No-name?" Sammy suggested on Monday. He and Charles were talking as they — and the rest of Mr. Mason's class — walked over to The Meadows to meet their Grandbuddies for the very first time. It was snowing again, just a little. Charles was hoping for a white Christmas. He liked it when there was enough snow for sledding during Christmas vacation.

"How would *you* like to be called No-name?" Charles answered. "Anyway, he has much too much personality for that. He needs a good name." Mom said they would know the right name when it came along. Charles hoped that would happen soon.

When they arrived at The Meadows, Charles suddenly felt shy. What were he and Mrs. Peabody going to talk about? As he and his classmates walked into the main building of the apartment complex, Charles tried to think of some topics. Mr. Mason had given them each a list of questions to "interview" their Grandbuddies with, but that wouldn't take long. His visit with Mrs. Peabody was going to last half an hour!

It turned out that he didn't need to worry about what to talk about. From the minute he and Mrs. Peabody met in The Meadows recreation room, they talked about dogs!

"I could tell from your letter that you love dogs," Mrs. Peabody said as soon as they sat down with their punch and cookies. She was a nice, smiley lady with white hair. She was wearing jeans and sneakers and a pin in the shape of a dog's head. "I love dogs, too!"

"Do you have one?" Charles asked. He was dying to tell her all about the new puppy, but he knew it was polite to ask questions first.

"Well, not anymore," said Mrs. Peabody. Her smile disappeared. "When I moved here a month ago, I had to give my dog to my daughter. He wasn't allowed to live with me at The Meadows."

"That's awful!" said Charles.

"He wouldn't have been happy here, anyway," said Mrs. Peabody. "He's a big dog, a Saint Bernard. He needs lots and lots of room. My apartment would have been much too small for Bruno. But I do miss him. I loved taking long walks with him every day. He was a good friend, and I could use a friend here. It's a little lonely, being the new person."

Charles knew how that felt. The Petersons had only moved to Littleton six months ago, and he had been very lonely until he became friends with Sammy.

Mrs. Peabody reached into her pocketbook and pulled out a photo album. "Here's Bruno at Christmas last year. Don't you love his Santa hat?"

Charles looked through all the pictures. Bruno looked like a great dog. He was really big — he came up to Mrs. Peabody's waist in the pictures! His white, brown, and black coat was beautiful, and he had a huge head with big, sad-looking eyes.

"I have a dog, too," he said. "At least — for a while." He explained about how his family was taking care of the Westie puppy until they could find him a good home.

"How wonderful!" said Mrs. Peabody. "You know, I had a Westie when I was a little girl. They need a lot of attention, but they are the smartest, dearest little dogs in the world." She smiled a little sadly. "Little Snowball. She was a trouble-maker, but I adored her."

"Snowball!" Charles said. "That's a great name. I wish we could find a name like that for this puppy."

"If you like the name, you can use it," said Mrs. Peabody. "It would be nice to know there was a new Snowball in the world." She smiled. "Although the first Snowball would probably throw a fit. She was known as the Queen of Maple Street, and she didn't put up with any nonsense from anyone."

"That sounds like our puppy!" said Charles, laughing. "He acts like a big dog, even though he's really little." Charles told Mrs. Peabody more about the funny puppy. As soon as the puppy had started feeling better, he decided he was boss of the whole house. If Lizzie didn't put his food dish down in exactly the right spot, he let her know it! He had a lot of energy, and he wasn't afraid of anything!

Charles was surprised when Mr. Mason came

to tell him that it was time to head back to school. He and Mrs. Peabody had been talking and laughing and having so much fun that the time had gone quickly.

"Bring me a picture of your puppy next time," said Mrs. Peabody as she walked Charles to the main door. "And wave when you pass by. That's my apartment on the corner right there," she said, pointing. "They tell me it looks out on the gardens in the summertime, but of course right now there's not much to see. Still, I like to sit by the window and watch who goes by."

Charles could tell that Mrs. Peabody was a little lonely. "I'll be back to visit soon," he promised. He gave Mrs. Peabody a hug.

"Oh!" she said. He could tell she was surprised. But then she hugged him back. "Good-bye, Charles," she said. "Take care of that little Westie!"

CHAPTER FIVE

"Snowball!" Lizzie called. She and Charles were playing with the puppy in the backyard after school. They were trying out the new name. The puppy came bounding over happily, his little tail sticking straight up in the air. He jumped up and put his paws against Lizzie's knee. "Oops," she said. "Down, boy. No jumping. No, no!"

The puppy was confused. Did the girl want him to run to her when she called or not? Why was she saying that "no" word? He didn't like that word at all.

Charles clapped his hands. "Here, Snowball!" he called. When the puppy came running over, Charles laughed. "He likes that name," he said. "It's perfect for him! He looks like a little snowball."

"He's going to look like a mudball soon," said Sammy. He and his dogs had just come over from next door, so the dogs could play together in the Petersons' backyard. "All the snow we got is melting. There's not even enough for a real snowball anymore." He sounded mad.

"At least it's warm enough to play outside," Lizzie said. "Let's see how everybody gets along."

Sammy's dogs ran over to sniff the little Westie pup. Rufus and Goldie seemed excited to meet a new friend.

"That's Snowball," Lizzie told them. "Be nice! He's just a puppy."

Rufus's tail was wagging — until the Westie jumped up and put his paws on Rufus's chest.

Snowball was so excited to meet two new friends. He thought he'd better let them know who was boss, right away.

"Snowball!" Lizzie cried. "No jumping on other dogs, either." She laughed. "That puppy isn't afraid of anybody. Rufus is so much bigger than him, but he doesn't care."

"Even Goldie is a lot bigger than he is — and they're about the same age!" said Charles. Now Goldie and Snowball were tumbling over and over in the muddy snow, mouthing at each other and growling little puppy play-growls.

First Goldie would be sitting on Snowball's head, then Snowball would be sitting on her head. Rufus stood a little way off, acting like the grown-up older dog he was.

Once in a while, Snowball would run away from Goldie and start to dig like crazy underneath the picnic table.

"Snowball's a terrier, all right," Lizzie said. "Terriers love to dig."

"I think that name is going to stick," said Charles. He thought about how happy that would make Mrs. Peabody. If only she could meet

Snowball! Maybe it would make her feel better about missing Bruno.

"I bet Mrs. Peabody would *love* to meet the new Snowball," he said. "It's not fair that dogs aren't allowed at The Meadows."

"But some dogs are," said Lizzie. "When my class was there I saw a sign about therapy dogs visiting every month."

"What's a therapy dog?" Sammy asked.

"It's a dog that goes around with its owner. They visit hospitals and nursing homes and anywhere that people need company or cheering up," Lizzie explained. "A therapy dog has to have good manners and special training, so it knows how to behave around sick people. I read all about them in my *Dogs on Duty* book."

Charles rolled his eyes. Lizzie was always reading about dogs. Then she explained every single fact she had learned. Still, this was interesting news. Charles had never heard about therapy dogs before.

"Rufus could be a therapy dog," said Sammy. "He has great manners."

"That's true," said Lizzie. "Goldie and Snowball could probably be therapy dogs, too. Then Snowball could visit Mrs. Peabody!"

"I like that name, but Snowball's not visiting anybody, looking like that," said Mrs. Peterson. Charles and Lizzy's mom had just come out into the yard with the Bean, and she was looking at the Westie puppy. "Didn't he used to be a *white* dog?"

Sure enough, the little Westie pup had gotten so muddy that he looked brown instead of white. Goldie was a mess, too.

"Now that you've named the puppy, maybe it's time to give him a bath," suggested Mom.

"Tubby!" cried the Bean. He loved bathtime.

"Can we give Goldie a bath, too?" Sammy asked. "She's as muddy as Snowball."

Mom started to shake her head. Then she shrugged. "Oh, why not? One puppy or two, how much difference could it make? It'll be a big mess either way." Charles knew that this was exactly the kind of thing that Mom didn't like about having a dog. But if he and Lizzie helped, maybe giving the puppies a bath could be fun.

They all went inside to get things ready. Mom ran warm water into the tub. Lizzie ran to the kitchen to get plastic cups for pouring water over the pups, and Charles got some old towels out of the rag bag. Sammy brought Rufus home, then took charge of keeping both puppies busy.

"We'll use the Bean's baby shampoo," said Mom, once they were all in the bathroom. "It's nice and mild." She glanced toward the door. "Let's make sure that door stays shut so the puppies don't get out."

Goldie watched with interest as everyone hurried around. Something great was going to happen! She could tell!

Snowball watched, too. Somehow he could tell that all this fuss was about him — which was how things should be. But he wasn't totally sure that this was a good kind of fuss.

"Let's get those pups into the tub." Mom took Goldie from Sammy's arms and gently lowered her into the water, which came up almost to her belly. Goldie didn't struggle at all. Her eyes were full of trust. She looked up at the humans, as if to say, "I'm sure you know what you're doing."

Then Mom picked up Snowball. He was not nearly as easygoing as Goldie. He stuck out his legs, trying to keep Mom from putting him in the tub, and let out a few barks.

The Bean laughed and barked back. "Tubby!" he cried again, leaning in to swish some water around.

"Stand back, Mr. Bean," Mom said. "Lizzie, can you hang on to the Bean? Snowball is having a hard time as it is." Finally, she lowered Snowball into the tub. Once he was standing in the warm water, he seemed to relax. "Great!" said Mom. "Okay, let's get scrubbing!"

The water in the tub had already turned brown from mud. It got even darker when Charles and Sammy used their cups to pour water on the puppies, wetting them all over. Then Sammy picked up the bottle of baby shampoo and tipped it over Goldie. "Whoops!" he said when he saw how quickly it came out. "Oh, well!" He began scrubbing as Charles poured some shampoo — a little more carefully — over Snowball.

Soon both dogs were all lathered up. "Now Goldie looks almost as white as Snowball!" Charles said. Goldie was covered in bubbles.

Mom let the dirty water out and ran some more. As Charles and Sammy began to rinse the squirming puppies, the phone rang. "I'll get it," said Lizzie. "Watch the Bean, okay?" She let herself out of the bathroom, carefully closing the door. A moment later, she yelled for Mom. "Phone!"

Mrs. Peterson wiped her hands on a towel. "Keep rinsing, boys," she said as she let herself out.

Sammy and Charles poured cup after cup of water over the puppies. It seemed to be taking forever to get all the bubbles out of their fur. Charles kept an eye on the Bean as he rinsed, but it seemed as if his little brother was busy playing with the bath toys that were lined up on the windowsill.

Then Charles turned to get some towels, and when he turned back, the Bean was in the tub — clothes and all — with the puppies. "Tubby!" yelled the Bean. "Wash doggie!" He poured a cup of water over his own head. Then he reached for Snowball.

"Oh, no," groaned Charles.

At that moment, Snowball scrambled out of the tub. The puppy shook himself off, splattering water all over.

"Oh, no!" groaned Sammy.

"What's going on?" asked Lizzie, opening the bathroom door.

Snowball took off, dashing through the door and down the hall. Water sprayed everywhere as he ran.

"Oh, no," groaned Lizzie.

Goldie scrambled out of the tub and took off after Snowball.

"Oh, no," groaned Mom, when she came in to see the Bean sitting alone in the tub, merrily pouring more water over his head. Snowball dashed by the bathroom door again, leaving a trail of water as Lizzie, Charles, and Sammy chased him.

It took over an hour to catch both puppies, dry them off, get the Bean dried off, and clean up the bathroom. By the time they were done, everyone was exhausted. But when Dad got home, he said Snowball looked — and smelled — great. Maybe it was worth it.

But Snowball had other ideas. Now he knew what "bath" meant. The chasing part was fun, but getting wet was not. Next time they tried to give him a bath, he would run and hide.

That night, Lizzie read about therapy dogs on the Internet. "Guess what?" she told Charles as they were brushing their teeth before bed. "The local therapy dog group is having a meeting next week. You can bring your dog in for a test. This could be the first step for Snowball to be a therapy dog! Then someday he could visit Mrs. Peabody."

Charles thought that sounded great. He knew Mrs. Peabody would love Snowball as much as he did.

CHAPTER SIX

Over the next week, Snowball kept getting healthier — and getting into more and more trouble! He chewed up one of Lizzie's soccer shoes. He tried to dig a hole in the living room rug. He dragged his food bowl all over the kitchen. You couldn't take your eyes off him for one minute. If you did, he would find something naughty to do!

But he was learning, too. Lizzie was training him a little bit every day, and he could already sit, lie down, and come when you called him.

On Thursday night, Dad drove Lizzie, Charles, and Snowball to the recreation center, where the therapy dog group was meeting. They found their way to the gym by following the sound of barking dogs. Snowball pulled at his leash. He wanted to be a part of whatever was happening.

"Wow, cool!" said Lizzie as they entered the gym. There were about six dogs milling around while their owners talked and watched them play. "Look, it's a Newfoundland," Lizzie added. She pointed to a huge, shaggy black dog.

Charles thought he looked as big as Mrs. Peabody's dog, Bruno.

"And a Pomeranian," Lizzie went on, pointing to a tiny golden dog, "and some kind of husky."

"Hello," said a woman in a green sweater, coming up to them. "You must be Lizzie Peterson. I'm Ms. Barrett. We spoke on the phone. Oh! And is this your dog?" She smiled at Snowball.

"That's Snowball," Lizzie said. "And this is my brother, Charles, and my dad."

When Snowball heard his name, his ears perked up. He ran toward Ms. Barrett and jumped up on her. "Snowball!" Lizzie cried. "No jumping!"

Ms. Barrett just laughed. "Why, he's just a puppy!" she said. "Unfortunately, dogs have to be at least a year old before they can become therapy dogs. They need basic manners and some obedience lessons, too."

Lizzie blushed. "We're working on that."

"Oh, I'm sure you'll do fine with him," said Ms. Barrett. "Westies learn fast. With just a little more training, he'll be a wonderful companion — and when he's older, he'll make a great therapy dog. Anyway, you're welcome to stay and watch. We're just having a little play time before we get started with our testing." She showed them where they could sit on the bleachers.

Charles was sad that Snowball could not become a therapy dog. Now the puppy wouldn't be able to meet Mrs. Peabody. Snowball seemed sad, too. He whimpered as he watched the other dogs play. "Poor buddy," Charles said, "you feel left out." He pulled a toy out of his pocket. "Here's your bone," he said, showing the rubber chew toy to Snowball.

"Want to play with this?" Snowball stopped crying and lay at Charles's feet, gnawing at the toy.

Suddenly, the big, shaggy Newfoundland came lumbering over and stuck his big nose right between Snowball's paws. Snowball jumped up and started barking, keeping the rubber bone under one paw. The Newfoundland backed off. The large dog stared at the puppy in surprise.

Snowball thought the older dog was silly. Did he think he could get away with taking the bone, just because he was big? Snowball barked a few more times, just to let the big dog know who was boss.

"Ha!" said Lizzie. "He thought he could steal the toy from Snowball. Boy, was he wrong!"

The Newfoundland's owner came running over. "Sorry!" she said. "Bear thinks all toys belong to him."

"That's okay," said Mr. Peterson. "Snowball thinks the *world* belongs to him!"

"Sounds like a terrier," said the Newfoundland's owner, laughing. "They're smart, but they can be a real handful with all that energy. They like to be in charge. Give me a big, goofy dog any day. They're much easier to deal with."

Charles didn't like to hear that, but Lizzie was nodding.

Just then, Ms. Barrett walked to the middle of the floor and clapped her hands. "It's time to get started with our testing," she announced. "For those who are visiting tonight, I'll explain a little about how this works. Basically, we are testing each dog for good manners, friendliness, and how well it behaves in public. A dog who can pass this type of test is known as a Canine Good Citizen, and he or she will receive one of these tags." She held up a little yellow collar tag. "To be a therapy dog, your dog will need to pass a few more tests as well. For example, we'll need to see how your dog reacts to a person in a wheelchair or someone using a walker."

Charles enjoyed watching the dogs go through

the test. Especially the Newfoundland. He was so calm and quiet. He walked nicely on a leash, let a stranger pet him, and didn't get scared when someone banged on a pot behind him. He also came when he was called, and let someone else hold his leash while his owner walked away. At the end, he got his Canine Good Citizen tag. Then he sailed through the therapy dog tests as well. The wheelchair didn't upset him, and he didn't seem to mind when Ms. Barrett pretended to have a huge coughing fit.

Charles saw Dad and Lizzie exchange a look. "Now, *that's* a dog," whispered Lizzie.

"Think you'll be able to do all that one day?" Charles whispered into Snowball's ear. It was too bad it would be so long before Snowball could be a therapy dog. Especially since Charles really wanted Mrs. Peabody to meet him!

The puppy wasn't sure what the question meant, but he knew how to answer. A big lick on the boy's nose meant yes, yes, yes!

CHAPTER SEVEN

Dear Santa,

How are you? You must be really busy right now with Christmas coming so soon.

My name is Charles Peterson, and I guess you already know that I have done my best to be very good this year. I haven't been perfect, I know. Sometimes I joke around too much in class, for one thing. But I'm trying.

One thing I have been really good at is taking care of dogs. Even Mom said I did a great job when we fostered Goldie, and I've been taking good care of Snowball, too. To me, this proves that I am ready to have a dog of my own. . . .

Charles knew that it was really up to his parents whether or not he got to keep Snowball. But he figured it couldn't hurt to put in a word with Santa as well. He had one last letter to write before Christmas vacation started. Why not make it a letter to Santa?

Charles had not quite finished his letter when the last bell rang, so he carefully put it into his writing folder. Then he jumped up and grabbed his jacket and backpack. Hooray! It was time to go home and see Snowball.

Hooray! The puppy was happy when he saw Charles come home. This had been the MOST BORING DAY EVER! But he liked this boy. Now that the boy was home, he would get to play!

Mom was really busy. She came downstairs to say hello to Charles, but then she had to get right back to work in her upstairs office. "Remember," she told Charles, "I'm working on an article. Dad and Lizzie and the Bean are off doing some Christmas shopping. So you're in charge of Snowball this afternoon."

Snowball looked up when he heard his name and cocked his head to one side. Charles bent down to give him a hug. He looked so cute when he did that.

"I know," Charles said.

"That means you have to make sure he gets some exercise," she said. "Maybe you could play in the backyard. He needs to burn off some of that energy."

Charles nodded. "Okay," he said.

"And keep an eye on him all the time," Mom reminded him. "I know he doesn't *mean* to get into trouble, but it seems as if every time I turned my back this week he was into something. He chewed on one of the Bean's favorite dolls. He dragged a pillow off the couch and all over the house. And he pulled half a roll of toilet paper into the kitchen."

Charles hid his face in Snowball's fur so Mom couldn't see his smile. He thought Snowball was pretty creative when it came to misbehaving.

"You know," said Mom, "I'm afraid that if we don't find a home for Snowball soon we may have to give him to the animal shelter. It might be easier to let *them* find him a home. He's a bit more than a family with three young children can handle. He really needs a home where he will have constant attention."

Charles stopped smiling. That sounded serious.

Snowball squirmed out of Charles's arms, then turned and gave him a quick lick on the nose before he charged off toward the living room.

"Better stick with him." Mom sighed. "In fact, go check that the door to the den is closed. I brought all the Christmas decorations and wrapping paper down from the attic and it's all in there. I don't want him getting into it."

"Don't worry, Mom," Charles said as he headed off after Snowball. "I won't let him out of my sight."

That afternoon, Charles and Sammy played with Snowball, Goldie, and Rufus for a long time in the backyard. More snow had fallen, so the dogs did not get muddy this time. In fact, there was enough snow to make snowballs and throw them for the dogs to fetch. All three dogs loved that game, but they were sometimes confused when the "ball" they were chasing seemed to disappear into a pile of snow.

When a snowball flew into a snowbank, Snowball would chase after it and then burrow deeper and deeper into the snow, trying to find it. The snow would fly between his little paws and his whole head would disappear into the hole he had dug.

When Sammy and his dogs went home, Charles and Snowball went inside to dry off and have another snack. Then Charles sat down at the kitchen table to make his Christmas list while Snowball curled up in a ball on the rag rug near the backdoor.

Dad

Mom

Lizzie

Bean

Snowball

Goldie

Rufus

Sammy

Gramma

That was a lot of people! Charles knew what he wanted to get his dad: a keychain shaped like a fish, since his dad liked fishing. And he had some pretty good ideas about dog toys. But what about everybody else? Presents were expensive. Charles wondered how much money he had saved up.

He glanced over at Snowball. The puppy was fast asleep. One of his legs was twitching a little, and Charles wondered if he was dreaming about running after Goldie.

Charles didn't want to wake Snowball up, so he

tiptoed out of the room and ran upstairs to get his Red Sox bank. He wanted to empty it out and count his money. It turned out there was a lot! He'd forgotten about the ten-dollar bill Gramma had given him for his birthday. That plus a whole bunch of quarters and other change turned out to equal almost twenty-three dollars!

Charles sat on his bed, looking at the piles of change. Maybe he could afford *two* dog toys for Snowball.

Snowball!

Suddenly, Charles realized that he had left the puppy alone. He shoved all the money back into his bank and ran downstairs, hoping he would find Snowball still curled up on the rug.

No such luck.

CHAPTER EIGHT

Charles dashed from room to room, looking for the puppy.

Snowball wasn't in the living room.

He wasn't in the dining room.

Then Charles heard a noise from the den. He smacked his head. "Oh, no," he groaned. He'd forgotten to check to make sure the door was closed. And guess what? It wasn't. Not all the way. With his heart thumping, Charles pushed the door open.

The puppy looked up at the boy. Why did he seem so upset? Snowball had never had so much fun in his life. He liked this room. There were so

many fun things to dig into, chew, and tear up.
What could be more fun?

Snowball looked like a Christmas tree that had gone through a blender. He had tinsel hanging off his ears, ribbons draped over his back, and a branch of plastic holly was stuck to his stubby little tail — which was wagging madly as he looked up at Charles.

"Oh, Snowball," Charles said. He couldn't help laughing at how cute the puppy looked. But then he got serious. The den was a mess! And it wasn't really Snowball's fault. He was only a puppy, and he didn't know any better. Charles knew he never should have left Snowball alone.

He scooped the little dog into his arms. "You're in trouble now," he said. "*I'm* in trouble now." How was he ever going to clean all of this up before dinnertime? Charles sighed and got to work.

56

Later that night, after dinner, Charles was looking at Lizzie's *Dogs on Duty* book. It was cool to read about all the things dogs could be trained to do: tracking lost people, doing police work, rescuing avalanche victims, and, of course, guiding blind people. There were even companion dogs who were trained to help disabled people with things like opening doors or picking up dropped keys.

"You could learn how to do those things," Charles told Snowball. He snuggled his nose down into Snowball's fur. "You could be a companion dog."

Then Charles thought about Mrs. Peabody. She was not disabled, but she certainly needed a friend. Wasn't that what a companion really was? A friend?

And Snowball needed a friend, too. He needed a friend who could give him lots of attention and take him for long walks and train him to do tricks and maybe even teach him to be a therapy dog. Charles knew his family was not a perfect fit for Snowball. They were too busy to watch him all the time. But maybe Snowball and Mrs. Peabody *were* a perfect fit.

The next day at school, Charles tore up the letter to Santa and started all over again with a new letter.

To the People in Charge at The Meadows,

My name is Charles Peterson, and my family is fostering a puppy named Snowball. He is a West Highland white terrier, and he is very smart and cute. And small. He has very good manners for a puppy, and he is learning very fast.

There is a lady who lives there named Mrs. Peabody. She is my Grandbuddy. I think she is lonely. She misses her dog. He was too big to live with her. But what about Snowball? He is just a little dog. He would be a perfect friend for Mrs. Peabody. And everybody else there would like him, too.

Why aren't dogs allowed at The Meadows? I think that stinks and you should change the rules. Then Mrs. Peabody could adopt Snowball and ~~I could visit him all the time~~. she would be happy.

Yours sincerely,

Charles Peterson

Charles finished his letter just in time. "Okay, everybody," Mr. Mason said, just as Charles was signing his name. "Time to clean up and get ready for our trip to The Meadows."

Charles folded up the letter and put it in his pocket. It was done, but he wasn't ready to send it yet. He wasn't completely ready to give up on the idea of keeping Snowball. And anyway, how could he be sure that Mrs. Peabody would really want to adopt a puppy?

Charles had such a fun time with Mrs. Peabody that day that he forgot all about the letter. They talked about all the things Snowball was learning to do. Charles told Mrs. Peabody about giving

Snowball a bath, which made her laugh so much that her face turned bright red. He also told her about watching the therapy dog test, and they both agreed that Snowball would make a great therapy dog someday.

The only thing they didn't talk about was Charles's letter. He decided to keep that a secret — for now.

Charles knew Mrs. Peabody liked dogs. He knew she liked Westies. But it was important to know whether or not she would really want to have Snowball for keeps. And there was only one way to find out for sure.

CHAPTER NINE

"Today's the day!" Charles whispered into the phone. It was Saturday morning.

"I'll be right over," Sammy whispered back.

The boys had been planning for days, and now it was time to put their plan into action. Snowball needed a walk. Mrs. Peabody needed a friend. And Charles wanted to make sure that Mrs. Peabody and Snowball would get along. So . . . why not walk Snowball over to The Meadows for a surprise visit?

It seemed like a good plan — as long as nobody found out, that is. And nobody would. Charles and Sammy had checked out the location of Mrs. Peabody's apartment, and they were pretty sure they could sneak Snowball in without a problem.

Just then, Mom walked into the kitchen with the Bean trailing behind her. He was wearing his favorite sweater, the red one with a black Lab knitted into the front. Snowball, still very white and fluffy, followed the Bean, snuffling up the crumbs from the Bean's graham cracker. The puppy had already learned that the Bean often dropped at least part of whatever he was eating.

"Who were you talking to?" Mom asked as she opened the fridge.

"Nobody," Charles said quickly. "I mean, just Sammy."

"And what are you two up to today?" she asked as she poured the Bean a cup of juice.

Charles looked down at his cereal bowl. "Nothing," he mumbled. "I mean, we're just going to hang out." He wasn't ready to tell Mom the truth about his plan.

* * *

The Meadows was a short walk from school but a longer walk from home. Or at least, it *seemed* longer to Charles and Sammy. Snowball was not used to walking on a leash. He pulled and tugged, checking out every single smell along the way. And he sniffed each one for a really long time, bracing his legs when Charles tugged a little on his leash. Charles tried to be patient, but finally he'd had enough.

"Come on, buddy," he pleaded when they had stopped for the twentieth time. He bent down and picked up the little dog, tucking him inside his jacket. Snowball struggled a little at first, then relaxed in the warmth of Charles's arms.

"Okay," Charles said as they neared the row of evergreens that grew between The Meadows and the road. "Anybody around?"

Sammy snuck a peek around a tree. "There's a guy shoveling his patio," he reported. "But he's looking the other way. Nobody else in sight!"

Charles took a deep breath. He and Sammy looked at each other. "Let's go for it!" said Charles. Holding tight to Snowball, he dashed across the snow-covered lawn to the sliding-glass doors of Mrs. Peabody's apartment.

"I sure hope she's here!" he said as he tapped on the glass.

The door slid open.

"Why, Charles!" said Mrs. Peabody, looking surprised. "How nice to see you!"

"This is Sammy," Charles said. Then he unzipped his jacket a little. "And this," he said, "is Snowball."

"Oh, my gracious!" said Mrs. Peabody, putting her hand over her mouth. "Oh, the little darling!" She leaned out the door and looked both ways. "Come in," she whispered. "A short visit won't hurt."

Once they were inside, Charles unzipped his jacket and let Snowball out. The little pup ran right over to Mrs. Peabody, who had knelt down with her arms open. She scooped him up and gave him a big hug.

"Oh, aren't you sweet," she said, nuzzling her nose into his fluffy, white fur. Snowball licked her nose. Then he licked her ears and her cheek for good measure.

The puppy knew this lady liked him. He could tell. He liked her, too. She knew just how to hold him so he didn't feel all squirmy, like he had *to get down right away. He wondered if she had any good treats. He licked her nose again.*

"He likes you," Charles said, laughing. "I can tell by the way he's licking your nose."

"My Snowball used to do that, too," Mrs. Peabody said. She looked happy and sad at the same time. She put Snowball on the floor and he took off, roaming around the apartment to check everything out. When he was done, he came back, sat down in front of Mrs. Peabody, and let out a few little barks.

"Shhh!" said Mrs. Peabody, putting her finger over her lips. "You're not supposed to be here, remember?"

Charles could tell that Mrs. Peabody knew exactly how to deal with Snowball's personality.

Snowball cocked his head and looked at her as if he understood.

But it was too late. A few moments later, there was a knock on the front door. "Hello-o!" called a woman, pushing the door open before Mrs. Peabody could stop her. "Did I hear a *dog* in here?" She spotted Snowball. "Oh, look!" she cried. "Isn't he adorable?"

Mrs. Peabody shrugged at the boys, smiling. "This is my next-door neighbor, Ms. Tucker," she said. "And this is Charles, and Sammy, and Snowball."

Charles held his breath. Was Ms. Tucker going to tell on them?

"Snowball," cried Ms. Tucker. "Come here, darling." She laughed as Snowball came trotting over with his stubby little tail stuck straight up in the air. Then she started talking baby talk to him. "Who's the little ittle boy?" she asked as she patted his head. "Who's the sweetest ittle puppy?"

Charles and Sammy looked at each other. The baby talk was silly, but they could put up with it — as long as Ms. Tucker didn't turn them in for sneaking a dog into The Meadows.

Mrs. Peabody and Ms. Tucker sat down on the couch with Snowball between them and started talking about dogs they remembered. Snowball just sat there, soaking up all the attention.

"Hello?" A man stuck his head through the door, which Ms. Tucker had left partway open. "I could have sworn I heard barking —" He stopped when he saw Snowball. "Hey there," he said, smiling.

"Now that's a fine pup." He came over to get a closer look. Then he called out the door, "Hey, Evelyn, come see what's in here!"

Before long, there were six residents of The Meadows surrounding Snowball.

"Look at him," Charles whispered to Sammy. "He's like a celebrity! And he loves it."

It was true. The puppy seemed totally happy being handed around from person to person, licking every nose he could reach. Charles remembered the therapy dog test and thought how easily Snowball could pass it. He knew just how to make everyone happy.

Mrs. Peabody looked over at the boys. Her cheeks were pink and she was smiling broadly.

Just then, there was another knock at the door. "Mrs. Peabody?" asked a woman in a white uniform, stepping into the room. "Sorry to bother you, but it's time for —"

"Hide him!" whispered Ms. Tucker, shoving Snowball toward the woman named Evelyn.

CHAPTER TEN

When they left, Charles let Sammy zip Snowball into his jacket. He had an errand to do. On the way out of The Meadows, at the reception desk, he dropped off the letter he'd written. Now he *knew* it was the right thing to do. Snowball and Mrs. Peabody belonged together.

"That was a close call!" Sammy said as he and Charles headed home with Snowball.

"But Evelyn really came through," Charles agreed. "I don't think that nurse suspected a thing." He looked down at Snowball, who was trotting happily beside him. "I have a feeling Mrs. Peabody is starting to make friends at The Meadows. What do you think, Snowball?"

Snowball cocked his head and wagged his tail.

The puppy had enjoyed meeting new friends. Those people seemed to understand that he should be the center of attention at all times. He liked that. He liked it a lot.

"Where have you been?" Lizzie demanded when Charles got home just in time for dinner.

"Out for a walk," Charles replied innocently. It was the truth, after all. He was tempted to tell Lizzie what a superstar Snowball had been at The Meadows, but it seemed best to keep that visit a secret for now. "How was Christmas shopping? Did you get me something good?" he asked.

"Guess you'll have to wait and see," Lizzie said.

Charles loved Christmas, but sometimes it drove him crazy wondering what presents he was going to get. He'd been asking for a dog every year since he could remember. But he'd never gotten one. Still, his parents and Santa usually came through with enough great presents that Charles wasn't too disappointed.

They all sat down at the table for dinner, and Mom had just started serving the macaroni and cheese when the phone rang.

"Hello?" Dad asked. He didn't like it when people called at dinnertime. "Well, yes, he's here. Just a minute." He put a hand over the phone and motioned to Charles. "It's for you," he said. "A Mrs. Collins, who works at The Meadows?" Dad looked curious.

Charles gulped. Had someone found out about Snowball's visit? He took the phone his dad handed him and cleared his throat. "H-hello?" he asked. "This is Charles." He walked into the living room so he could talk privately, in case he was in big trouble.

A few minutes later, he came back into the

kitchen, hung up the phone, and burst out with a cheer. "Yes!" he cried.

"What is it?" asked his mother. "Something about your Grandbuddy?"

"Sort of," Charles said. "It's about Snowball, too. I think I've found him a home!"

He explained everything. It turned out that small dogs *were* allowed at The Meadows, as long as they were well-behaved. Mrs. Collins wanted to come over and meet Snowball. She wanted to make sure he was the kind of dog that would fit in at The Meadows.

"So she'll be here in half an hour!" Charles finished.

"What, tonight?" his mother asked.

Charles nodded. "I want to give Snowball to Mrs. Peabody for Christmas. There's no time to waste!"

His mother threw up her hands. "Okay, everybody. Let's finish our dinner quickly and then you can all help tidy up a bit."

The next twenty minutes went by in a blur of

activity. Charles had never eaten dinner so quickly. Then he helped clear the table, took Snowball out for a bathroom break, and helped the Bean round up the toys and books that were scattered all over the living room. Meanwhile, Mom and Dad and Lizzie were running around, too.

When the doorbell rang, Mom smiled at Charles and gave him a high five. "Good job!" she said.

Mrs. Collins turned out to be a really friendly woman who didn't even blink when the Bean barked at her. She just patted his head and said, "Nice doggy."

After they had talked for a while, Mrs. Collins finally said, "So, where *is* this puppy I've heard about?"

Dad looked at Mom.

Mom looked at Charles.

Charles looked at Lizzie.

They all looked at the Bean.

The Bean barked again and laughed his googly laugh. He was no help.

"Where *is* he?" Mom asked.

"I took him out after we ate," Charles said. "But then we were all running around . . ."

"Oh, no!" Lizzie gasped. "I just remembered. I was tidying up in the den, and I saw him come in. When I went out, I must have closed the door so he wouldn't get into the Christmas wrapping stuff! Only I — I closed him in *with* it."

Charles groaned. He could just picture what that room was going to look like. By now, Snowball had probably shredded every bit of wrapping paper into big, wild, colorful piles, and draped ribbons all over the furniture.

When Mrs. Collins saw that mess, she was *never* going to let Mrs. Peabody adopt Snowball.

"I guess we'd better go find him," Dad said grimly. They all followed him as he led the way to the den and opened the door.

"Aww," sighed Mrs. Collins when she looked in. "What a darling!"

There were no wild piles of shredded wrapping paper.

No ribbons draped from wall to wall.

There was just fluffy white Snowball, all curled up in a little nest of red tissue paper. He opened one eye and thumped his tail when he woke to see everyone looking at him.

Snowball couldn't understand why everyone was laughing. What was all the fuss about? He had no idea what was so funny. He was just trying to take a nap.

Charles could hardly wait until Christmas. He and Lizzie worked hard on Snowball's training. The puppy learned so fast! Now he could walk on his leash without pulling, shake hands, and fetch his toys from a basket. On Christmas Eve, they gave him another bath so that he was as white and as fluffy as he could be.

Finally, the big day arrived. Charles and his family arrived at The Meadows. This time, there was no sneaking. Snowball walked proudly along with them on his leash, with a huge bright red bow tied around his neck.

"Surprise!" Charles shouted when Mrs. Peabody answered her door. "Merry Christmas! Do you like your present?"

He knew she did, even though she was crying.

Later, when Charles gave Snowball one last hug before they left, he thought about how much he had wanted to keep the fluffy little puppy for himself. But he also knew that Snowball had found the best home in the world.

Snowball and Mrs. Peabody were a perfect match. Someday, Charles would find his *own* perfect match. Someday, the Petersons would find the right dog at the right time. But until then, there would always be puppies who needed homes. And Charles and his family would always be happy to help each puppy find the perfect place.

PUPPY TIPS

Caring for your puppy includes taking it to the vet for regular checkups, not just when it is sick.

What else does caring for a puppy include? Here is a list of daily tasks:

- Feed your puppy.
- Give it fresh water.
- Keep its bowl clean.
- Walk your puppy.
- Spend some time training your puppy.
- Groom your puppy's coat.
- Check your puppy's eyes, ears, paws, and mouth.
- Love your puppy!

Puppies are a lot of work, but they are worth it. Are you ready to take care of a puppy?

Dear Reader,

My dog's name is Django. (The D is silent, so you say it "Jango.") I was so proud of him on the day he passed his Canine Good Citizen test. A well-behaved dog is a pleasure to be around. Django does not jump up on people, bark at them, or bite.

He knows how to do lots of things! He will sit, stay, be friendly with other dogs and people, and come when called. He also walks nicely on a leash, shakes hands, and waves "bye-bye." He can even eat an ice-cream cone in ten seconds flat! What a good boy.

Yours from the Puppy Place,
Ellen Miles

P.S. For another brave pup that was nursed back to health, read LUCKY.

THE PUPPY PLACE
Where every puppy finds a home

LUCKY

ELLEN MILES

SCHOLASTIC